TOGORIAN TRAP

This galaxy is yours.
Be a part of

#1 *Assault on Yavin Four*
#2 *Escape from Thyferra*
#3 *Attack on Delrakkin*
#4 *Destroy the* Liquidator
#5 *The Hunt for Han Solo*
#6 *The Search for Grubba the Hutt*
#7 *Ithorian Invasion*
#8 *Togorian Trap*

. . . and more to come!

#8

Togorian Trap

DAVE WOLVERTON

SCHOLASTIC INC.
New York Toronto London Auckland Sydney

ISBN 0-590-12992-9

12 11 10 9 8 7 6 5 4 3 9/9 0 1 2 3/0

Printed in the U.S.A.

First Scholastic printing, April 1998

Preliminary Mission

CHAPTER 1

"This is it," Han Solo shouted. "I'm going to get those bounty hunters once and for all — before they get us. Luke, Leia — get to the gun bays. Chewie — put full power to our forward shields."

There was a worried beep from the droid Artoo-Detoo, who was back on the forward observation deck. His fellow droid, See-Threepio, calmed him down, saying, "I wouldn't worry about Master Solo. He knows what he's doing. I just hope there aren't any droids aboard that vessel."

Solo hit the thrusters and hurtled toward the small ship that had just dropped out of hyperspace. The ship was a Corellian JumpMaster 5000 and it was aiming to attack the *Falcon.* Solo knew the model well. More important, he recognized this *particular* ship as one that had fled the Ithorian system only a few days ago. It had some modified weapons systems, but it was still much weaker than the *Falcon.* The pilot had clearly been relying upon a surprise attack. But Solo was ready.

Behind Solo, Grubba the Hutt slithered down the hall. Seeing the ship on the monitor, Grubba shouted, "Wait! You can't blow that ship — those guys still owe me a gambling debt!"

"Sorry, Grubba," Solo said. "You'll just have to find someone else to cheat."

Solo navigated toward the oncoming ship. The other pilot hesitated, no doubt attempting to power his shields and weapons.

A moment was all Solo needed. He broadcast a tight-beam message to the enemy ship: "Hate to do this to you buddy, but you've been on my tail for weeks!" He hoped that the message wouldn't be picked up by any Imperials. His location, planet Togoria, was mighty close to an Imperial shipyard.

The bounty hunters fired a blaster cannon — five or six shots in rapid succession. The *Falcon* bucked as its shields took the impact.

Solo fired his ion cannon, and the smaller vessel was immediately enveloped in a web of blue lightning. The electric bolts wriggled over the hull of the ship, magnetizing its sensors, destroying its circuitry, and ruining its weapons tracking systems. A perfect hit.

"Yeeeeoooooowww!" Grubba shouted. "That fried them!"

Solo got a sinking feeling. He knew the despair and horror the bounty hunters must be feeling. Their ship was a tomb. Even the escape pod would be useless.

They wouldn't be able to communicate or flee. Their life-support systems would go down. They would either freeze in the depths of space or, if the ship was captured by Togoria's gravity, they would burn up as the ship plunged through the planet's atmosphere.

The bounty hunters only had one slight chance: In a matter of minutes, they would have to de-ionize the ship, make the necessary repairs, and escape the tomb.

The chance that the bounty hunters would hear his final words was very slim, Solo knew. The ion blast would probably have fried the circuitry. "So long," Solo whispered into his communicator. "Sorry it had to end this way. But it's either you or me."

"Sorry it had to end this way." The words were a hissing sound through the crackle of static. Yet from the inside of his ship, Dengar heard Solo.

He already had his de-ionizer in hand, and was desperately struggling to clear the static electricity from his operations console. From the back of his ship, he heard the cries of Udin the Kubaz and Eron Stonefield. The *Punishing One*'s hull was blown wide, and bits of shrapnel had burst through a containment wall. The cabin was quickly losing air. Udin had applied a patch to the hole, and was now sealing it with durofoam. Unfortunately, the artificial gravity had been deactivated, causing Udin to float away from the job.

"Give me a hand here, when you can!" Dengar shouted.

"How about giving us a hand when *you* can!" Eron yelled. She was trying to help Udin. "If we can't breathe, it doesn't matter if we can fly!"

"And I really don't care if I'm breathing when I crash into the planet!" Dengar shouted. He turned back to the console. It was hopeless. Far too much work, far too little time.

At that moment, the air pressure punched through Udin's patch. The hole was too big. The thin metal twisted and flew through the hole. The air in the cabin was escaping.

"Quick, this way!" Dengar shouted. He unstrapped himself from the pilot's seat and kicked toward the escape pod.

"What good will that do?" Eron cried as she and Udin moved toward the door. With the escape pod ionized, they wouldn't be able to eject from the ship. They might have a little more air, but they'd still crash.

Eron and Udin flew through the weightless air like ghosts, and entered the tiny round hatch of the pod.

Just then, a minor explosion rocked the ship. Eron locked the hatch down, inhaling gratefully.

"I'm glad you got us in here!" Udin cried in relief.

There were no lights in the escape pod. Dengar held up his de-ionizer, and worked by the dim glare of its little green running lights.

The escape pod didn't have many controls. A tiny electronic brain managed the life support and the jets. The brain wasn't smart. It only knew to fire its thrusters and keep the craft from crashing. It would also try to fall on even ground, rather than hard rocks — *if* it had any choice in the matter.

The *Punishing One* began to shudder. Eron knew the feeling: the ship had hit the atmosphere of a planet.

"We're going to burn up on entry!" Udin cried.

Eron bit her lip and looked out the view port. She saw the *Millennium Falcon* veer away. Below was a beautiful planet — a jewel with sapphire-colored oceans, a few emerald jungles, and tawny plains, all obscured by sunlight reflecting off of clouds. "We've lost the *Falcon*," she reported. "At least they won't be tailing us anymore."

Dengar was sweating and straining, running the de-ionizer over the delicate controls. Suddenly, a single green running light shone on the control panel.

Eron read the words under the light. "Parachutes —

automatic deployment." She gasped in relief. The parachutes could slow their descent. This might give Dengar time to get the jets running, or at least control the crash.

Dengar rushed for a handle at the bottom of the escape pod and pulled it. Eron covered her ears to block out the grinding sound of metal against metal. Then she felt the pod float away from the body of the *Punishing One*. Not far — only a few feet.

The escape pod twisted so that sunlight showed through the hatch and lit Dengar's face. Eron could see enormous beads of sweat on his brow as he kicked back toward the computer console and resumed the de-ionization.

"We need these thrusters!" he muttered.

As the ship rushed through the upper atmosphere, the friction of metal against air heated the skin of the ship. It began to get very hot.

"Can you get the life support working?" Udin pleaded. "I need fresh air."

"We've got enough," Dengar shouted. "We'll crash before we run out of oxygen."

"Perhaps you have enough for a human," Udin argued, the voice from his translator sounding tinny, "but I am a Kubaz. I feel . . . faint."

With that, the Kubaz's eyes rolled up in his head. His tiny trunk wriggled up in the air, then went limp.

"You *look* faint," Eron said.

Udin pitched forward, unconscious.

Dengar grunted, trying to focus on getting the controls to work.

The fall to Togoria stretched out for minutes. The escape pod rolled and tumbled with seeming slowness toward the planet. Within the pod, gravity returned slowly as they fell.

Eron watched Dengar work with unswerving determination, touching the de-ionizer to each tiny circuit and component under the maintenance panel. She searched desperately for a way to help.

There was a booming noise and a sudden lurch as the automatic parachute deployed.

Within moments, the pod began swinging by the lines of its parachutes. But that wasn't enough to make Eron feel safe. By now the escape pod felt like an oven. And it was only getting worse.

"Just a moment," Dengar muttered to himself. "I've almost got it. I've almost got it."

Eron looked out the hatch, just as a blanket of clouds rushed toward them.

The pod slowed, but not enough. If it hit ground, Eron knew that they'd explode into a bloody spot on the rocks.

Dengar shouted, "Just about! I just about have it!"

Eron was suddenly blinded, as the ship descended through clouds. Gray fog obscured her view.

Then they were beneath the clouds, plunging toward the jungle.

Regretting she had ever become a bounty hunter, Eron Stonefield screamed.

CHAPTER 2

The city of Caross, the capitol of Togoria, was a marvel to behold. Leia had never imagined anything like it, though she had long had relations with the Margrave's sister, Ffaseer effet Ihsss. The Margrave-sister secretly supported the Rebellion. Her people could not bear the thought of being ruled by the Empire. Unfortunately, the nearby Imperial shipyards made it hard for the Togorians to openly rebel.

The Togorians seldom invited aliens to their world, but Leia found that when she asked for permission to land, the response was overwhelming. The Margrave-sister herself spoke on the comm console. In a leathery, purring voice, she invited Leia and the others to be royal guests in Caross.

Soon they were winging toward the city. The plains around Caross were a brown savanna of tall grass, with a few watering holes and enormous trees. The land was dotted by herds of shaggy dark creatures that looked (and sometimes acted) like living hills. Giant flying reptiles called mosgoths hunted overhead.

The catlike Togorians had evolved strangely. The plains of Togoria could be dangerous, with the reptiles hunting above and the vicious predators on ground. And the shaggy creatures would crush anything that moved beneath them.

The Togorians' ancestors had sought refuge in the trees during the day, and hunted at night. Hidden in the upper branches, they were shaded from the burning sun and shielded from reptiles. Even now, the nomadic Togorian males still camped in trees.

The females preferred not to wander, and had built cities where they could bear their litters in peace. Each city was located near a nesting site for mosgoths. By living with these creatures, the Togorians had learned to protect themselves from some of their enemies.

The city of Caross looked like a grove from a distance. Its brightly painted domes shone like jewels on platforms built into enormous sandstone-red trees.

Grubba the Hutt watched the skyline warily. "Let's not go there," the young Hutt groaned at last. "I'm afraid of heights."

"It's really not too dangerous," Solo said, "as long as you mind your manners. I hear that the Togorians have a rule with unwanted guests: they invite them to leave by dragging them to the edge of the city and throwing them off."

Grubba's yellow eyes widened. Then the young Hutt slithered away — closing the hatch with a slam.

Leia shook her head, wondering if it was wise to frighten the Hutt. After all, Grubba came from a powerful family.

On the platforms, Leia could see aviaries where mosgoths perched. Some of the giant reptiles were ridden by Togorian girls with gray pelts and enormous fangs, who carried heavy blasters on their hips. As the *Falcon* neared Caross, the mosgoths swarmed after the ship.

Solo veered toward the largest landing pad and settled the ship down in what looked to be a market square. A sun-dappled village squatted beneath the platforms. Togorian females herded their litters of "kits" everywhere along the streets. Various stalls sold fresh fish, reptiles, and mammals for food.

Leia stepped from the *Falcon* first. In Togorian society, it was customary for women to lead. After Leia came See-Threepio, to translate, followed by Artoo-Detoo. Last of all came the males.

There were few adult male Togorians in the capital. They were considered too wild for polite company.

Leia walked into the sunlight. Everywhere she could smell the scents of fresh meat — dark shaggy etelo and the slender forms of giant silver bist. She looked up, and saw the pelts of leathery foora, large green lizards, drying in the sun like enormous green leaves.

Almost immediately, the Margrave-sister bounded toward her. The Sister's black claws were retracted, a sign of peace. Leia folded her hands to hide her fingernails — the best she could do to show her own peaceful intentions. The Sister's pelt was a charcoal gray, with a streak of white between the eyes. The diamond-shaped pupils in her red eyes narrowed to slits in the sunlight. She stood a full head taller than Leia, though she was only half the height of a Togorian male.

"Welcome, Leia of the humans," the Margrave-sister purred. "I hear you shot down a ship?"

"Imperial bounty hunters," Leia said. "They'd been following us for weeks."

The Sister's whiskers twitched, and her triangular ears went backward. She hissed, claws flexing, "After what your friends did to the Death Star, I am not surprised. Still, you need not fear Imperials here. You are my royal guests."

With merely seconds remaining, Dengar hunched over the control panels, trying to save his hide.

The escape pod hurtled into the upper branches of the jungle, shearing through the canopy. The first few small branches barely slowed the vehicle, and then it smashed into a limb. Metal buckled beneath Dengar's feet, and a great wedge of wood drove through the metal fabric of the escape pod. For half a second, he hoped that the branch would support the pod, but quickly the branch was torn away, and the pod dropped another dozen yards. The parachute tangled wildly in the branches and began to tear. The pod lurched sideways, and Eron Stonefield fell to the floor with a grunt.

Then the pod bounced in midair. The parachute jostled and swayed, swinging wide. Dengar felt sick to his stomach. He feared the parachute lines would rip the rest of the way, dropping the pod who-knows-how-far.

But the pod held.

Dengar's heart hammered. The Imperial physicians who had turned him into an assassin, who had cut away that portion of his brain that allowed him to feel love and compassion, had also cut away his ability to feel fear.

He was not frightened now. Yet his heart hammered, and a sheen of sweat was on his brow. Some deep part of him still knew fear. It was mingled with another emotion, one that the physicians had left in him.

Rage. A seething rage that burned like a coal in his belly. He told himself silently, *I will have vengeance. I will have Solo.*

CHAPTER 3

The jungles of Togoria proved forbidding even to Dengar and his comrades. The trees blotted out nearly all light, and everywhere on the flat ground were bogs and pools of quicksand. Dengar had never seen a snake over a hundred feet long until he tried to climb over what he'd thought was a log. Lightning fast, it moved to strike. Dengar dodged out of the way just in time, coming way too close to its oddly triangular head and its trio of venomous fangs.

Dengar did not have any idea where he was going. He and the other bounty hunters stumbled along through thick, strange-smelling moss. The odor numbed his nose and tongue, as if the moss had emitted a mild sleeping gas to repel any herbivores that might try to feed on it.

Dengar pulled a bandage from his neck to cover his nose. Then he turned back to look at the others. Eron Stonefield was already half asleep on her feet, while Udin — awake now — seemed not to be bothered by the gas at all. Sometimes it paid to be an alien.

Dengar took one last look at the *Punishing One* — amazingly, it had not been destroyed in the crash. But it would need plenty of repairs before it flew again.

Dengar's thoughts were disturbed once more by the odor. Just as Dengar realized that he had to get away from the moss, an enormous gray shape dropped to the ground in front of him. He saw the cat's eyes in the dark — then the raking claws, the twitching whiskers, and the long teeth oozing spit. The Togorian landed almost silently on its padded feet.

The tall creature sniffed him and hissed, "What are you doing here, human?"

"Hunting snakes," Dengar answered.

"You are not a white-shell. You are not a stormtrooper. What are you?"

Dengar knew that the cat people hated the Empire. "I'm not an Imperial, but I've killed a few of them," he boasted casually.

"It is forbidden for humans to land on Togoria," the cat-man said.

Eron Stonefield cut in. "Our ship crashed."

Dozen of Togorians leaped from the trees, falling like huge fruit. "It is lawful to crash —" the Togorian said, "— but you may crash only once. We will take you to Caross, where freighter pilots will dispose of you. If you ever crash on our world again, it would be less painful to die in the crash than to fall into our hands."

"I am in a hurry," Dengar told the Togorian leader. "I am hunting a man who will be in Caross for only a few hours."

The Togorian raked the air with giant claws. "So you are a human who hunts other humans," the Togorian mused. "Interesting. We are hunters, too, though we do not hunt our own kind."

"This man is a criminal," Dengar said.

"On Togoria, the mighty rule. Might is law. This way is best."

"I am mightier than this man," Dengar stated. "He is evil. He has stolen an alien child, and demands a ransom."

The Togorian snarled. "He stole a mother's kitten?"

Dengar smiled. Male Togorians were not allowed to run loose in the cities. He suspected that when they did go to the cities, honor would demand that they behave. "Such men dishonor all males everywhere. The human's name is Han Solo. He has the child, and will try to sell it in Caross."

"Such human creatures should not live," the Togorian proclaimed. "I am Fassool, leader of this war band. We will fly to Caross on mosgoths, and find this human. When we find him, we will tell the Margrave-sister. She will cut him to pieces!"

"No," Dengar insisted. "When we find him, you must give him to me. We must take him alive, and make certain no harm comes to the child. They're worth more alive than dead."

Fassool shook his head. He argued that the Women's Clan would handle the matter.

Dengar knew the Togorians would not help him if they knew the whole truth about Solo. The Togorians wouldn't harm a Rebel hero, especially one who was only trying to collect the reward on a child he'd rescued.

Yet if Dengar, Eron, and Udin were to find Solo and his Rebel cronies, they would need the Togorians' help. Somehow, Dengar hoped to win their support.

Mission Briefing

Before you proceed, you must consult the Mission Guide for the rules of the STAR WARS MISSIONS. You must follow these rules at all times.

This is a Bounty Hunter mission.

While tracking down Han Solo and his Rebel allies, you have crashed on the planet Togoria. You and your fellow bounty hunters have enlisted the aid of some Togorian males to lead you to the city of Caross. You must try to win their respect and allegiance before you get there, so that you can use them to find Solo and the other Rebels. In Caross, you must capture Han Solo so that you can get the bounty on his head. You must also recapture Grubba the Hutt, to get the reward for the child.

You start this Mission with the Mission Point (MP) total from your previous Mission. If this is your first Mission, you start with 1,000 MP.

Choose your Bounty Hunter character now.

You take a stun baton, plus two other weapons of your choice.

For a vehicle, you will ride a mosgoth. The giant flying lizards are the only mode of travel available in a society that has little technology.

You can use Power three times on this Mission.

Good Luck.

Your Mission:
Togorian Trap

Fassool and the Togorians begin to lead you through the swamp. Because they stand tall and have enormous legs, they run with incredible swiftness, often falling to the ground and racing on all fours when climbing gentle hills.

They make a game of racing ahead of you, mocking your "stubby legs" as you desperately race to keep up through the jungle. Each time you come to a giant snake, you must spring over it. At your touch, the snakes look back. The first couple of times that you leap, you are close behind the Togorians, and the snakes do not bother you. They know better than to mess with Togorians.

But after awhile, you begin to tire.

You rush up to another giant snake, and leap. The snake rears up, three green eyes glaring at you intently. A long red tongue flickers out to taste the air.

Then the snake strikes at you, venomous teeth flashing in the air like sabers.

You must choose to evade, hypnotize, or fight the snake.

To evade the snake: Your stealth# +1 is your confront#. Roll the 6-dice to evade the snake.

> *If your confront# is equal to or more than your roll#,* add the difference +3 to your MP total. You leap around some trees and lose the snake in the jungle. You may now proceed.
>
> *If your confront# is lower than your roll#,* subtract the difference from your MP total. The snake has spotted you with its three eyes. You must fight it (below).

To hypnotize the snake (using Power)*: Choose your Hypnotism Power. Your charm# + your Power's low-resist# + your Power# is your confront#. Roll the 6-dice.

If your confront# is equal to or more than your roll#, add the difference +3 to your MP total. The snake is lulled into complacency. You may proceed.

If your confront# is lower than your roll#, subtract the difference from your MP total. The snake isn't falling for your spell. Now you must fight (below).

Note: This counts as one of three Power uses you are allowed on this Mission.

To fight the snake: Choose your weapon. Add your weaponry# to your weapon's mid-range# +3 for your confront#. Roll the 12-dice to shoot the snake.

If your confront# is equal to or more than your roll#, add the difference +2 to your MP total. The smell of fried snake fills the forest, and makes you hungry. You may now proceed.

If your confront# is lower than your roll#, subtract the difference from your MP total. Add +2 to your confront# for your new confront#. Repeat this confront with the same new confront# until the snake is defeated.

Your efforts at confronting the snake cause you to fall behind the others. Distantly, you hear the Togorians meowing and hissing with catlike laughter, calling to you.

It bothers you that the Togorians think so little of you. You need the big males to help you capture Solo. Certainly, Solo and the others will be well-protected by their friends at Caross.

You begin to consider ways that you might impress the Togorians. As you do, you finally exit the jungle and come to the savanna. Ahead of you is a small, wide river that flows lazily over the dry flatlands. Its banks are muddy and wide, and you can see that they have been flooded recently.

A herd of reptiles are drinking at the water's edge. The reptiles look like small tyrannosaurs, possessing tan-colored hides with dark stripes. These little meat eaters terrify you, yet you see that they eye the Togorians nervously. As long as you are with the Togorians, you will be safe.

When you finally catch up with the Togorians, they smile at you. "We must cross the river," Fassool says. "It will be dangerous."

"Why?" you ask. "Are there reptiles in the water? Carnivorous fish?"

"Nothing so pleasant —" a Togorian answers. "There are . . . mud worgs."

"*What* is a mud worg?!"

Fassool shrugs. "If you have not seen them, I cannot say."

You wonder what he means, and the Togorians move forward. They halt when they come to the muddy banks of the river.

Without warning, one of the Togorians leaps into the mud and begins racing over the mud flats. You hear a high, buzzing noise, like an electric saw, and see movement in the mud. Something small is under the sloppy mud, something perhaps a half meter across. It begins racing through the mud at incredible speed, chasing the Togorian. You can't see the creature itself, only the wake of the mud moving above it.

Suddenly, the buzzing stops. A long white tooth pokes up from the mud. As the creature rushes silently along, the jagged tooth cuts through the mud like the fin of a shark cutting through water. You know that if it reaches the Togorian, the mud worg will slice his foot in two.

You draw your blaster, preparing to shoot the mud worg.

To shoot the mud worg: Choose your weapon. Since this is a small target, add your weaponry# to your weapon's long-range# +2 for your confront#. Roll the 12-dice to aim and fire.

> *If your confront# is equal to or more than your roll#,* add the difference +7 to your MP total. It's a perfect hit.
>
> *If your confront# is lower than your roll#,* subtract the difference from your MP total. Add +2 to your confront# for your new confront#. Repeat this confront with the same new confront# until you have blasted that worg out of the mud.

The Togorians all laugh at you. One of them says, "It is a good thing that you shoot faster than you run, little human. But please, do not ruin our sport. It shames a male to need rescue from a mud worg."

As the Togorian runs through the muck, you see another mug worg rise silently from the brown ooze. The white tooth on its back races toward the Togorian. When it looks as if it will hit, the Togorian deftly leaps into the air. The mud worg passes beneath him harmlessly, and all of the Togorians laugh and applaud.

The Togorian races out into brown water. It cannot be more than six centimeters deep, since his feet hardly get wet as he crosses the wide river.

Other mud worgs are hiding in the water by the dozens — the Togorian appears to be dancing as he races through them, leaping and twisting each time a tooth slashes at his foot. In some cases, when the mud worgs are racing fast and furious, the Togorian pulls out his blaster and shoots one.

When a mud worg lands a strike, the Togorian's blood splashes in the air. The other Togorians break out in raucous laughter, shouting, "One point for the mud worgs!"

This does not stop the Togorian. In moments he is across the river, on the far side of the mud. He waves a hand, urging others to cross.

Fassool looks down at you. "Well, little friend, it looks as if it is your turn."

"What . . . happens if I slip in the mud?" you ask.

"Then the mud worgs will slash you to pieces, and dine on your flesh beneath the mire."

You know that you must earn the respect of the Togorians. Taking a weapon in each hand, you leap through the air.

When you hit ground, the mud is thick and slippery.

To avoid falling in the mud (without Power): Your skill# +1 is your confront#. Roll the 6-dice to keep from slipping.

If your confront# is equal to or more than your roll#, add the difference +3 to your MP total. Only your feet are muddy.

If your confront# is lower than your roll#, subtract the difference from your MP total. You land in the mud, and the Togorians laugh at you as you climb quickly to your feet. You wish you had claws on your feet, like the Togorians. It would make things a lot easier.

To avoid falling in the mud (using Power)*: Choose your Balance Power. Your skill# + your Power's low-resist# + your Power# is your confront#. Roll the 6-dice.

If your confront# is equal to or more than your roll#, add the difference to your MP total. You've made it safely through.

If your confront# is lower than your roll#, subtract the difference from your MP total. You land in the mud, and the Togorians laugh at you as you climb quickly to your feet. You wish you had claws on your feet, like the Togorians. It would make things a lot easier.

Note: This counts as one of three Power uses you are allowed on this Mission.

You race ahead. On the far banks of the river, the mud worgs turn — you see brown muck moving in their wake as they race toward you. The Togorians begin to cheer and shout. Some of them hold up necklaces with claws or other trinkets, shouting out bets as to whether you'll live.

Ahead of you, a mud worg suddenly rises from the river, a white tooth slicing through the muck.

You can shoot the mud worg or you can try to dodge it.

To shoot the mud worg: Choose your weapon. Add your weaponry# to your weapon's close-range# +3 for your confront#. Roll the 12-dice to shoot the mud worg.

> *If your confront# is equal to or more than your roll#,* add the difference +5 to your MP total. Bits of mud worg fly everywhere. You may now proceed.
>
> *If your confront# is lower than your roll#,* subtract the difference from your MP total. Add +2 to your confront# for your new confront#. Repeat this confront using the same new confront# until you have gotten rid of this predator.

To dodge the mud worg: Your stealth# +2 is your confront#. Roll the 6-dice to jump in the air and avoid the mud worg.

> *If your confront# is equal to or more than your roll#,* add the difference +2 to your MP total. You have deftly leapt over the charging mud worg.
>
> *If your confront# is lower than your roll#,* subtract 5 MP from your MP total. The mud worg nicks you as it passes. Proceed.

Your feet hit water, and you dance to the side. The mud worgs feel your vibrations through the ground — each time your feet land, they adjust their course.

Three more of them slice toward you, each from a different direction. You try to fire on two of the mud worgs as you evade the other.

To evade a mud worg while firing on others: Add your weaponry# to your weapon's short-range# and your stealth# +3. This is your confront#. Roll the 12-dice.

> *If your confront# is equal to or more than your roll#,* add the difference +7 to your MP total. You may proceed.
>
> *If your confront# is lower than your roll#,* subtract the difference from your MP total, and repeat the confront until you have been successful.

You land in the mud. Ahead the mud worgs are so thick that you doubt you'll make it to the far bank. But you realize that if they are attracted to you because they feel your vibrations, then they can be fooled.

You reach down and grab a mud worg that the Togorian killed. The creature has an enormous, thorn-shaped bone on its head; six flippers along its bottom to propel it through the mud; and a short, thick tail. Its mouth is a horror — a gaping cavern filled with sharp teeth.

You throw the dead creature far away from you. It hits the mud with a splat.

The other mud worgs scythe toward it, hitting the dead creature and slicing it in pieces.

As they pass, you rush forward.

Four mud worgs buzz back toward you.

You race through the slippery mud to escape them, trying to place your feet without raising a wake.

To escape (without Power): Your stealth# + your skill# is your confront#. Roll the 6-dice to escape from the last of the mud worgs.

> *If your confront# is equal to or more than your roll#,* add the difference to your MP total. It's amazing how fast you can run when you're terrified. You may now proceed.
>
> *If your confront# is lower than your roll#,* subtract 5 MP from your MP total. The mud worgs try to slice through your good solid boots. You retreat and must try again. Repeat the confront until you make your escape.

To escape (using Power)*: Choose your Balance Power. Your skill# + your Power's low-resist# + your Power# is your confront#. Roll the 6-dice.

> *If your confront# is equal to or more than your roll#,* add the difference to your MP total. It's amazing how steadily you can run when you're terrified. You may now proceed.
>
> *If your confront# is lower than your roll#,* subtract 5 MP from your MP total. The mud worgs try to slice through your good solid boots. You retreat and must try again. Repeat the confront until you make your escape.

****Note:*** This counts as one of three Power uses you are allowed on this Mission.

For surviving the mud worgs, reward yourself 30 MP (60 MP for Advanced Level players).

You reach the far bank, and the Togorians all cheer and clap. Some of them pay off their bets with daggers and necklaces. Then another Togorian tries to cross the river.

This Togorian carries no weapons, and seems exceptionally agile. He dances through the mud, a huge smile on his face, letting the mud worgs narrowly miss him. His every action seems to say, *This is how it should be done.*

But when he reaches the water, he steps on a sinisterly hidden mug worg. Its toothlike fin punctures his foot, rattling and tearing as it comes out of the water.

The Togorian roars. As he tries to kick the monster away, he slips helplessly in the mud. In a heartbeat, a mud worg slices through his thick leather vest — the Togorian falls backward with a yowl. The mud worgs pounce upon him, dragging him deeper into the mud as they feed.

The Togorians scowl at their friend's misfortune. But at least they can now walk across the mud without fear. The mud worgs' hunger has been safely satisfied.

You run on into the night. You are more weary than you've ever been. Still, the Togorians push you onward.

You cross the plains, reaching a fetid swamp. The water here is unnaturally warm. You smell the stink of sulfur rising from the ground. All around, Togorian trees have died. Their twisted trunks rise up, weird dark limbs curled in the air.

The ground beneath your feet is spongy, and you ask the Togorians if there are mud worgs around.

"No," one of your hosts answers. "The water here is too hot for them. This is the Swamp of Vapors."

Steam rises from the ground in dozens of places where hot water is vented from the ground. The strong Togorians use rags to cover their noses. Their ears lie back in anger, and their stubby tails twitch.

"Aagh," Fassool gasps. "I can take this stench no longer. We are leaving."

With that, he pounces away, running ahead in the darkness. The other Togorians turn to you, annoyed. "You humans are slow as kittens," one says. "We cannot stand to breathe this stench any longer. We will wait for you on the far side of the swamp. Beware the vapors in this place."

Without another word, the Togorians lope off. You wrap a scarf tightly about your face. The stench of sulfur is strong, but it doesn't really bother you. You wonder if the Togorians simply have a strong and sensitive sense of smell.

You march through the night vapors, among the burning pools. The fog becomes so dense that you cannot see. As you stumble in the darkness, wreathed in mist, you feel an odd sensation: something soft, almost a whisper of air, brushes your leg.

You leap up, and make out a dim light. There is a creature here, glowing the palest shade of white. It has long tentacles wreathing out from a central body that you can see right through. The creature is clearly made from some kind of gas!

The Togorian's warning rings in your ears — *Beware the vapors!* A long tentacle brushes up your back, and another twists in front of your face. The gaseous creature seeks an opening to your body. If it gets into your lungs, you fear you will choke to death.

You open your mouth to shout for help — and the glowing tentacle tries to force its way in!

You can try to dodge the mist creature or fight it.

To dodge (with Power)*: Choose your Evasion Power. Your Power# + your Power's mid-resist# + your stealth# is your confront#. Roll the 6-dice to evade the mist.

> *If your confront# is equal to or more than your roll#,* add the difference +5 to your MP total. The monster lunges for you, but you're already gone. You may proceed.

> *If your confront# is lower than your roll#,* subtract the difference from your MP total. The mist continues its attack, and you must fight it (below).

****Note:*** This counts as one of three Power uses you are allowed on this mission.

To dodge (without Power): Your stealth# +2 is your confront#. Roll the 6-dice to dodge the mist.

> *If your confront# is equal to or more than your roll#,* add the difference +3 to your MP total. You dodge the mist and leap away. You may now proceed.

> *If your confront# is lower than your roll#,* subtract the difference from your MP total. The mist seeks to enter your mouth and nostrils. You must fight (below).

To fight: Choose your weapon. Your weaponry# + your weapon's close-range# is your confront#. Roll the 6-dice to fight the mist.

If your confront# is equal to or more than your roll#, add the difference to your MP total. The heat of your weapon seems to puncture the mist, causing a glowing gas to escape the beast with a hissing sound. You won't have to worry about it anymore. You may now proceed.

If your confront# is lower than your roll#, subtract the difference from your MP total. You are choking. Subtract 1 from your confront# for your new confront#. Repeat the confront using this new confront# until you have destroyed the mist creature.

You stumble away from the mist, watching intently for more of these monsters. Several times, you see the pale glow above hot pools. You avoid these places at all cost.

You run through the swamp. Hot pools are all around, and eventually you run out of ground to walk on. The only way across the burning water is a trail of giant slip pads. In order to cross the swamp, you must leap from slip pad to slip pad. And you must be careful — around the slip pads, you see the glowing forms of mist creatures.

You must leap across the pads as silently as possible, with or without power.

To cross the burning water (using Power)*: Choose your Balance Power. Your strength + your Power's low-resist# + your Power# is your confront#. Roll the 6-dice.

If your confront# is equal to or more than your roll#, add the difference +2 to your MP total. You silently hop past the gathered monsters. You may now proceed.

If your confront# is lower than your roll#, subtract 4 MP from your MP total. The mists detect your presence and come searching for you. You must escape using an alternate route. Repeat this confront until you escape the mists and cross the burning water.

Note: This counts as one of three Power uses you are allowed on this Mission.

To cross the burning water (without Power): Your stealth# + your strength# is your confront#. Roll the 6-dice to evade the mists.

If your confront# is equal to or more than your roll#, add the difference +3 to your MP total. You silently leap past the gathered monsters. You may now proceed.

If your confront# is lower than your roll#, subtract the difference from your MP total. The mists detect your presence and come searching for you. You must escape using an alternate route. Add +1 to your confront# for your new confront#, and repeat this confront using the new equation until you escape the mists.

You pass the mist creatures, but find that the farther you go into the water, the farther apart the slip pads become, until you can barely see the next one from where you stand. Perhaps if you were a Togorian, this would not pose such a challenge. But you do not possess the Togorians' skill at leaping. You reach a point where it will require all of your strength to leap between the pads. You draw a weapon, just in case the mist creatures appear. Choose your weapon now.

To leap to the next pad: Your strength# is your confront#. Roll the 6-dice to leap.

If your confront# is equal to or more than your roll#, add the difference +7 to your MP total. You leap easily to the new pad. You may now proceed.

If your confront# is lower than your roll#, subtract the difference from your MP total. You fall into the burning water with a loud splash. You climb out quickly, with only minor burns. But your weapon has been damaged — you must have knocked it when you landed. You must try to repair it (below).

To repair a damaged weapon: Your skill# +1 is your confront#. Roll the 6-dice to repair the weapon.

If your confront# is equal to or more than your roll#, add the difference to your MP total. The weapon might be a little bent up, but it works fine. You may now proceed.

If your confront# is lower than your roll#, subtract the difference from your MP total. You'll have to work on this one at home, where you've got the proper tools. Remove this weapon from your arsenal for the remainder of this Mission.

You continue to leap from slip pad to slip pad. Through the fog ahead you see land, and on the shore you see a large creature — like a giant woolly pig, with enormous curved tusks. As you approach, it rapidly transforms into a creature that looks exactly like the Togorian leader, Fassool! Then it morphs into a snarling mass of teeth and fur.

Spotting you, the creature leaps. You may evade the creature, put it to sleep using Power, or fight it.

To evade the monster (without Power): Your stealth# +2 is your confront#. Roll the 6-dice to evade the monster.

If your confront# is equal to or more than your roll#, add the difference +5 to your MP total. You easily dodge the monster and hide from it in the brush. You may now proceed.

If your confront# is lower than your roll#, subtract the difference from your MP total. The monster chases you, towering over your head. You must fight (below).

To put the monster to sleep (using Power)*: Choose your Sleep Power. Your Power# + your Power's low-resist# + your stealth# is your confront#. Roll the 6-dice.

If your confront# is equal to or more than your roll#, add the difference +4 to your MP total. The creature sleeps so soundly, you wonder if it will ever wake up. You may now proceed.

If your confront# is lower than your roll#, subtract the difference from your MP total. The monster chases you, towering over your head. You must fight (below).

****Note:*** This counts as one of three Power uses you are allowed on this Mission.

To fight the monster: Choose your weapon. Your weaponry# plus your weapon's mid-range# +4 is your confront#. Roll the 12-dice to fight the monster.

> *If your confront# is equal to or more than your roll#,* add the difference +6 to your MP total. The monster takes a hit and goes rushing off into the dark. You may now proceed.
>
> *If your confront# is lower than your roll#,* subtract the difference from your MP total. The monster rushes you. As it does, it morphs into a perfect image of . . . you. Now you must fight this evil twin (below).

To combat your monster duplicate: Your weaponry# + your weapon's close-range# + your stealth# +3 is your confront#. Roll the 12-dice.

> *If your confront# is equal to or more than your roll#,* add the difference to your MP total. You watch in horror as you see yourself fall wounded. For a moment, you forget you are seeing a duplicate. Then the creature begins to morph into its original state, hairless and evil. It staggers and dies.
>
> *If your confront# is lower than your roll#,* subtract the difference from your MP total. You must try again. Add +1 to your confront# for your new confront#. Repeat the confront using the same new confront# until you have defeated the horrific duplicate.

That wasn't easy. Reward yourself with 30 MP (40 MP for Advanced Level Players).

You climb a small hill, drawn to the raucous laughter of Togorians. They've been watching you from afar. Fassool smiles, his teeth flashing beneath the light of three pale green moons. You wonder if it is really Fassool, or if the being in front of you is also some kind of monster.

"So, little human," the Togorian says, "you do not look so happy to see me. Does my appearance not please you?"

"What was that creature back there?"

"The shaper? That particular breed is called a Toothsome Image, since it has far too many teeth. But there are other species of shaper on Togoria, too. Be glad that you didn't meet something more horrific. Now, while we wait for your friends, we must call our mosgoths. Help us pull out this fire bush."

The Togorians point at some small bushes. You grasp a bush and pull at it. The roots are deep, but when you twist the trunk it pulls out easily. The Togorians pull out a dozen similar bushes and lay them down in an odd shape — a bar with wings on one end and an arrowhead at another. They set fire to the bushes, which burn with an amazing green, smoky flame. They also sputter and crackle, causing you to realize that they must be filled with some sort of alien salts.

Together the fires create an odd hieroglyph of flame. You wait patiently, and soon an enormous flying reptile lands just outside the fire. The creature stands ten meters tall, and has a wingspan of forty meters. Its green scales reflect the firelight, and in the darkness it is a creature of profound beauty, glittering like millions of emeralds, with onyx horns curling backward.

A Togorian races up to the giant reptile and pats its snout affectionately. You realize that this must be a mosgoth. It must have been feeding recently, for dried blood crusts its lips and teeth. The mosgoth nuzzles the Togorian, who loops a halter of thin rope over the beast's head.

In moments, more mosgoths begin to drop from the sky. You see them wheeling overhead, shadows in the moonlight until they drop. They stand around your little group, silent winged giants.

Fassool warns you, "Take care with your mount. The mosgoths are wild creatures, and a bit clumsy. They may step on you by accident."

"Wild?" you ask. "But aren't these *your* mounts?"

"They are not ours," the leader answers. "Mosgoths belong to the sky, and to themselves, just as Togorians belong to the trees. But for generations we have built our camps near their nesting grounds, and protected them from their enemies. So they have learned to respect us, to understand some of our tongue, and to treat us as allies. We are not friends to them, merely allies in the battle for survival on our harsh world. Perhaps someday, a thousand generations from now, we will earn their friendship. But for tonight, we are merely allies. These mosgoths are well fed, and have consented to fly us to Caross.

"You must hang on tight," Fassool warns. "The beasts are anxious tonight."

You climb onto the back of a mosgoth, as the Togorians begin to snarl directions to their mounts. There isn't any saddle — the only thing to hold onto is a thin cord of rope.

You cling tightly to the mosgoth with your legs, and grab the rope with all your strength.

As the Togorians take off, your mosgoth bounds forward in three great steps, bouncing so hard it jars your bones.

To keep from falling off the mosgoth: Your strength# +1 is your confront#. Roll the 6-dice to hang onto the mosgoth.

> *If your confront# is equal to or more than your roll#,* add the difference to your MP total. You cling to the mount as it takes to the sky.
>
> *If your confront# is lower than your roll#,* subtract the difference from your MP total. The monster dislodges you, and you must climb back on immediately (below).

To climb back on: Your skill# + your strength# is your confront#. Roll the 6-dice.

> *If your confront# is equal to or more than your roll#,* you've climbed back on. Now you must keep from falling off again (above).
>
> *If your confront# is lower than your roll#,* subtract the difference from your MP total. Not good enough! Repeat this confront until you have climbed back on.

With a great rush, the mosgoth takes to the sky. You feel the wind in your face, and hear the pulsing air beneath your mount's wings. With a throaty cry the mosgoth rises up toward the moons, as you gaze all around, amazed.

You fly for what seems like a long time. A warm front blows in, bringing clouds and a light rain. The rain is icy on your face, and it makes the scales of your mosgoth slick. The Togorians begin shouting to your mount, urging it higher up into the clouds.

A bolt of lighting flashes nearby, and the peal of thunder shakes you. You hear a startled cry, and see that one of the other mosgoth's wings has been torn by a bolt of lightning. Both the creature and its Togorian passenger plummet through the rain toward the ground, thousands of feet below.

You rise above the clouds, into the gentle glow of moonlight. The three small green moons hang in the sky, and their light reflects from the tops of clouds.

Suddenly, you hear a throaty roar. At first you think it is thunder once again, and then you realize that no — it is the sound of something living. The Togorians shriek in terror — "Liphons! Liphons are after us!"

Something enormous blots out the sky above you. Your heart races. The Togorians — who had until now seemed so fierce — feel fear.

The enormous flying monster dives toward you with a roar. Its wings blot out the moons and the clouds. Other batlike liphons flicker behind it, wheeling in the night.

Your mount cries out a challenge and opens its mouth, baring enormous teeth that gleam in the darkness. Stealthfully, it climbs toward its attacker. The liphon dives, its jaws opened wide. You have no choice but to fight.

To fight the liphon: Choose a weapon. Your weaponry# + your weapon's long-range# +4 is your confront#. Roll the 12-dice.

If your confront# is equal to or more than your roll#, add the difference +10 to your MP total. It was a perfect hit. The limp form of the liphon falls away in the darkness, and you hope it doesn't fall on someone below. You may now proceed.

If your confront# is lower than your roll#, subtract the difference from your MP total. The liphon draws closer. Add +1 to your confront# for your new confront#. Repeat this confront using the same new confront# until the liphon plummets.

Other liphons are attacking your allies below. You see a liphon hurtle toward a Togorian and sweep him from his mount with the claw at the end of its wing. There is nothing you can do for the hapless Togorian but to battle on. Nearby, Fassool is fighting for his life. As he grapples with one of the liphons, another wings toward him from behind.

You must save him.

To save the leader of the Togorian band: Choose your weapon. Your weaponry# + your weapon's long-range# +1 is your confront#. Roll the 6-dice.

If your confront# is equal to or more than your roll#, add the difference +5 to your MP total. With shooting like that, you should probably consider entering the galactic tournaments. You may proceed.

If your confront# is lower than your roll#, subtract the difference from your MP total. Repeat the confront until you blow this liphon from the sky.

For defeating the liphon, award yourself 60 MP (85 for Advanced Level players).

The liphon drops into the darkness with a shriek. Fassool looks up and catches your eye. He knows that you may have just saved his life.

His own mount rips a hole in the second liphon's wing, and Fassool is face to face with the monster when he finally brings it down.

"Retreat into the clouds!" he then shouts.

The mosgoths dive with a cry of rage and defeat.

Soon you find cover in a dense fog.

You hear wounded Togorians grunting and crying out. One of them raises a dim red light, to show his companions where he is in the fog, and in moments the others do the same. They begin to talk in their hissing language.

After a few moments, Fassool says to you, "You hunters have fought well. There are those among us who owe you our lives. What boon would you have as payment?"

Now is the moment, you realize. You want his support.

"The man Han Solo must be taken to justice," you say. "I fear that your Margrave-sister will cut him to pieces, but if I get him to justice alive, I will get a large reward. Help me catch him."

Fassool studies your face from afar. "This is a hard thing you ask," he says. "The Margrave-sister rules in the city. It would not be lawful."

"Your clan is mighty," you answer. "Did you not say that on Togoria, the mighty rule?"

You know you must persuade Fassool to help you without question. Choose now whether to use Power.

To persuade Fassool and his clan (without Power): Your charm# +1 is your confront#. Roll the 6-dice.

If your confront# is equal to or more than your roll#, add the difference to your MP total. Your arguments seem wise to Fassool, and he pledges to help you.

If your confront# is lower than your roll#, subtract the difference from your MP total. Fassool is no fool. Though he owes you his life, he takes more persuading. Repeat this confront until you have him thoroughly convinced.

To persuade Fassool to follow you (using Power)*: Choose your Persuasion Power. Your Power# + your Power's medium-resist# + your charm# is your confront#. Roll the 6-dice.

If your confront# is equal to or more than your roll#, add the difference to your MP total. Fassool would gladly lay his life down for you. You may proceed.

If your confront# is lower than your roll#, subtract the difference from your MP total. Repeat the confront until Fassool is convinced.

Note: This counts as one of three Power uses you are allowed on this Mission.

Blinded by your persuasive powers, Fassool says, "For your acts of heroism this night, we will give you aid in your hunt. We of the Mindnight Fire clan promise this."

This news makes you optimistic. There must be a dozen Togorians in this band, and they will be a great help in your fight against Han Solo. He and his Rebel outlaws are as good as captured. . . .

After some time, your mounts descend from the mist once more. Below, the world is a moonlit sea of fog, and in the distance you see the lights of a city. After a bit of study, you realize the city is resting on a series of platforms made of stone, shaped like an enormous tree.

"Caross," Fassool growls. "We are almost there. It is good that most of the city is under cover of the clouds."

Within seconds, your flight of mosgoths drops down, spiraling into the fog to land on a platform in the city.

You prepare yourself for a jarring landing.

To avoid being thrown from your mount upon landing: Your strength# + your skill# +4 is your confront#. Roll the 12-dice.

> *If your confront# is equal to or more than your roll#,* add the difference +4 to your MP total. You now ride as if you were born on a mosgoth. The landing is no problem.
>
> *If your confront# is lower than your roll#,* subtract 10 MP from your MP total. You pitch forward on the first bounce and land on the ground. You are bruised, but not seriously hurt. You pick yourself up and rejoin the Togorians.

The Togorians rapidly hold counsel. As they sit, growling and yowling to one another, you take stock of the city. Tall buildings of stone are everywhere, and many windows shine with dim lights. You see some Togorians moving about on a nearby platform, perfectly at ease while walking in this foggy night.

"Any humans in the city will be under royal guard," Fassool says. "The palace is not far. But you visitors will attract attention. Come with us, but try not to be too noisy. We have landed downwind from the royal apartments, so we do not have to worry about your stench alerting the guards. The fog will conceal most of our movements, but it would be best if you removed your loud footwear."

The Togorians are fortunate enough to have thick pads on their feet, and they walk very silently.

"I don't like the idea of trying to walk barefoot on streets of stone in the dark," you answer back. "Don't worry about me, I'll keep quiet."

The Togorian shakes his head. "As you wish."

He looks pointedly at your weapons. "Set your weapon to stun. We wouldn't want to kill any female Togorians by accident."

You draw your weapon and follow the Togorians into the foggy night. They send scouts ahead to watch your path. They lead you through seemingly deserted buildings and out onto an industrial plaza where bales of cloth and crates of unknown goods form a maze.

Near the palace — a tall building with royal spires like needles at the top — your guide halts. "It will be much harder from here," he warns.

The Togorians climb on some crates to get a better look at the palace. You notice the *Millennium Falcon* on a docking platform below you and to your right. The gangplank on the spaceship is down, and the working lights are on, as if someone is making repairs. A Wookiee lugs a portable welder down the gangplank and heads to the nose of the ship. Moments later, Solo himself walks down from the gangplank and shouts, "Chewie, quit messing around with that and give me a hand in here. I need some muscle on this wrench."

Chewbacca roars and follows Solo into the *Falcon*. You can see at least six Togorian guards outside the ship — two along a bridge between the palace platform and the loading platform, and another four stationed outside the ship. These guards are easily as large as the Wookiee.

You nudge Fassool and point to the ship, wondering how to surprise the guards. Fassool growls low in his throat, and points to a platform far below you. The other Togorians study it and nod.

The drop must be at least a hundred yards down. You wonder if the Togorians can handle such a fall.

Nervously, you follow them back through the maze of boxes. They stop near some bales of rope and begin measuring out lengths. You suddenly understand their plan.

"See that pole?" Fassool asks.

On the end of the platform is a pole with a winch that can be used to transfer goods to the lower platform.

"Yes," you answer.

"Tie the ropes to it. The guards will be less likely to spot a small creature like you. Still — be careful."

You take the ropes and sneak to the lip of the platform. The pole is on the very edge. You must tie the ropes to the pole without being noticed.

To tie the ropes to the pole: Your stealth# + your skill# is your confront#. Roll the 6-dice.

> *If your confront# is equal to or more than your roll#,* add the difference +7 to your MP total. You manage to tie a few granny knots without being spotted.
>
> *If your confront# is lower than your roll#,* subtract the difference from your MP total. One of the guards glances up — you must stop tying and hunch down for a moment. Repeat the confront using the same equation until the knots are tied.

The ropes are secured in such a way that you can't really climb down — you have to grab the rope and swing to the platform below. If the ropes are cut too short, you're going to have a rough fall when you try to swing down to the next platform. And if the ropes are cut too long, you will splat on the pavement.

Worried, you crawl back to the Togorians.

When you are all ready, Fassool says to you, "This is your fight. It is only right that you take the place of honor — at the front of the battle."

Grabbing your weapon, you run sideways, and leap into the darkness.

You hurtle downward. As you reach close to the ground, you realize that the ropes are cut too short.

To land safely, you must either seek to cushion the blow by using Power or use your strength.

To land (using Power)*: Choose your Object Movement Power. Your Power# + your Power's low-resist# + your strength# is your confront#. Roll the 6-dice.

If your confront# is equal to or more than your roll#, add the difference +7 to your MP total. You gently float to the ground.

If your confront# is lower than your roll#, subtract the difference from your MP total. The landing was a bit jarring, but you'll be okay.

Note: This counts as one of three Power uses allowed on this Mission.

To land (without Power): Your strength# +2 is your confront#. Roll the 6-dice.

If your confront# is equal to or more than your roll#, add the difference +11 to your MP total. You swing down flawlessly.

If your confront# is lower than your roll#, subtract the difference from your MP total. You swing down and land with a thud. Ouch!

You roll to your feet near a Togorian guard. She turns and reaches for her weapon.

You may try to put her to sleep using Power, stun her with your weapon, or fight her hand-to-hand.

To put the guard to sleep (using Power)*: Choose your Sleep Power. Add your Power# to the Power's mid-resist#. This is your confront#. Roll the 6-dice.

If your confront# is equal to or more than your roll#, add the difference + 6 to your MP total. The guard falls asleep, purring like a kitten.

If your confront# is lower than your roll#, subtract the difference from your MP total. The guard snarls and draws for her weapon. You must stun her or fight her hand-to-hand (below).

Note: This counts as one of three Power uses you are allowed on this Mission.

To stun the guard: Your weaponry# plus your weapon's close-range# is your confront#. Roll the 6-dice to shoot.

If your confront# is equal to or more than your roll#, add the difference +5 to your MP total. Maybe a stunner isn't as fancy as Power, but it can be just as effective.

If your confront# is lower than your roll#, subtract the difference from your MP total. The guard swings her claws at you and knocks your weapon to the ground. Now you must fight hand-to-hand (below).

To fight the guard hand-to-hand: You better hope size doesn't matter — the guard definitely has the height advantage here. Your strength# + your stealth# +4 is your confront#. Roll the 12-dice.

If your confront# is equal to or more than your roll#, add the difference +10 to your MP total. The bigger they are, the harder they fall.

If your confront# is lower than your roll#, subtract the difference from your MP total. The guard lands a body blow. You have to rally here. Add +1 to your confront#

for your new confront#. Repeat the confront using this new confront# until you have triumphed.

In the darkness behind you, a Togorian male lands on his feet and bounds forward. He lunges at another nearby guard, and in moments they are struggling.

You see the streaks of blaster bolts as the guards begin shooting. One of the Togorian males falls lifelessly from his swinging rope.

At that moment, Han Solo shouts from the hatch of the *Falcon*, "Hey, what's all the noise out there?"

He sticks his head out of the hatch, sees you, and shouts, "Chewie, get us out of here!" He's already turned around and running up the gangplank when you hear him add, "We got company."

The gangplank to the *Falcon* begins to close, and its auto-cannon drops. You don't want to take a stray round, and you're not about to let Solo escape!

You rush for the gangplank, and try to leap inside the *Falcon* before the door closes.

***To leap into the* Falcon:** Your strength# + your stealth# is your confront#. Roll the 6-dice.

> *If your confront# is equal to or more than your roll#,* add the difference to your MP total. You slip into the ship just as the hatch closes.
>
> *If your confront# is lower than your roll#,* subtract the difference from your MP total. The door begins to clamp shut on your foot. Repeat the confront until you make it inside.

You make it under the door in the nick of time. As you do, you find a golden droid in the hall before you. "Oh, my!" he shouts. "Bounty hunters!"

You must either shut him down or shove him aside.

To shut down the droid: Your skill# +2 is your confront#. Roll the 6-dice.

If your confront# is equal to or more than your roll#, add the difference to your MP total. The light in the droid's eyes goes dim, and he slumps forward.

If your confront# is lower than your roll#, subtract the difference from your MP total. The droid swats at you with his metal hands and shouts, "Oh, oh, get away from me!" In frustration, you decide to shove him aside (below).

To shove the droid aside: Your strength# +2 is your confront#. Roll the 6-dice to knock the droid down.

If your confront# is equal to or more than your roll#, add the difference to your MP total. The droid falls over and shouts, "How horrible! We droids seem to be made to suffer!"

If your confront# is lower than your roll#, subtract the difference from your MP total. The droid grapples with you, shouting, "I've got him, Master Luke! Help me, Artoo!" Repeat the confront until you can knock this golden droid to the floor.

A small astromech droid rolls up to you. You decide to leap over it.

To leap over the small droid: Your strength# +1 is your confront#. Roll the 6-dice to hurdle over the droid.

> *If your confront# is equal to or more than your roll#,* add the difference to your MP total. This droid makes an excellent hurdle. You may proceed.
>
> *If your confront# is lower than your roll#,* subtract the difference from your MP total. You knock the droid as you come down, and land clumsily on the other side.

You run further within the *Falcon*, up a short corridor. You don't want any Rebel scum sneaking up behind you, so you dart left, to make sure the crew's quarters are clear.

As you run into the quarters, you see Grubba the Hutt sitting at a gaming table. On the other side of the table is a handsome young man with sandy blond hair.

Grubba glances up at you and says, "It's about time you showed up. Life with Rebels is boring!"

The young man jumps up and shouts, "Han, in here!" He reaches to draw a lightsaber from his side.

Your fire your stunner, and the young man twists his wrist. The lightsaber ignites and blocks the bolt.

"I'm coming, Luke!" Solo shouts.

You are face-to-face with Luke Skywalker, the Rebel pilot who blew up the Death Star.

What a reward you'll get for this catch!

"I give you your choice," Luke says. "Surrender . . . or die!"

"And I'll not give you any choice, Skywalker," you answer with a smile. You raise your stunner and begin to fire rapidly. He blocks the blaster bolts in an amazing display of prowess.

You may seek to put Luke Skywalker to sleep using Power, run defense by using Object Movement Power, or shoot him with your stunner.

To put Skywalker to sleep (using Power)*: Choose your Sleep Power. Add your Power# to the Power's high-resist# +3 for your confront#. Roll the 12-dice.

If your confront# is equal to or more than your roll#, add the difference +15 to your MP total. Skywalker drops like an anvil.

If your confront# is lower than your roll#, subtract the difference from your MP total. Skywalker warns, "The light side of the Force is more powerful than the dark." You must stun him (below).

Note: This counts as one of three Power uses you are allowed on this Mission.

To penetrate Skywalker's defense while shooting (using Power)*: Choose your Object Movement Power. Your Power# + your Power's high-resist# +3 is your confront#. Roll the 12-dice.

If your confront# is equal to or more than your roll#, add the difference +15 to your MP total. Skywalker's lightsaber goes flying from his hand. You fire your stunner into him at point-blank range, and Skywalker goes out cold.

If your confront# is less than your roll#, subtract the difference from your MP total. Skywalker hardly misses a beat as he grabs the lost lightsaber in mid-air, then swings at you. You must now fight with your stunner (below).

Note: This counts as one of three Power uses you are allowed on this Mission.

To fight Skywalker with your stunner: Skywalker advances on you, swinging his lightsaber. You fire as you retreat. Choose your weapon. Your weaponry# plus your weapon's short-range# +3 is your confront#. Roll the 12-dice to fight Skywalker.

If your confront# is equal to or more than your roll#, add the difference +7 to your MP total. Luke misses and takes a hit to the ribs, dropping with a stunned sigh. You may proceed.

If your confront# is lower than your roll#, subtract the difference from your MP total. Repeat the confront until Luke is stunned.

Even though the young Jedi is down, you don't want to take any chances with him. You pull some restraints from your belt and begin to cuff him.

Grubba shouts, "Hey, let me do that!"

"Go ahead, worm," you answer. Grubba hurries forward and begins to secure Skywalker.

You hear the trace of a footfall and glance behind you. The beautiful Princess Leia Organa is rushing toward you while loading a blaster.

You realize that your own weapon needs to be reloaded. You decide to knock her weapon aside.

To disarm Leia: Your strength# +1 is your confront#. Roll the 6-dice.

> *If your confront# is equal to or more than your roll#,* add the difference + 3 to your MP total. Leia's weapon goes spinning away.
>
> *If your confront# is lower than your roll#,* subtract the difference from your MP total. Repeat the confront until Leia drops her weapon.

You point your own weapon at Leia and say, "Give it up, Princess, or when this blaster bolt takes your head off, it will mess up your hair real bad!"

At that moment, a brilliant flash of red light whips past your shoulder. The blaster bolt tears open an access panel. You hear the scream of rending metal. Molten fragments fly everywhere.

Leia takes advantage of the distraction by trying to escape.

You move to restrain her.

To restrain Princess Leia: Your strength# + your stealth# is your confront#. Roll the 6-dice.

If your confront# is equal to or more than your roll#, add the difference to your MP total. Princess Leia won't break free again. You may proceed.

If your confront# is lower than your roll#, subtract the difference from your MP total. Luckily, the princess doesn't get far — at least not far enough to find a weapon. You move to restrain her again. Repeat this confront until you have done so.

Chewbacca roars in anger, and you throw yourself to the floor just as another flash of red shoots overhead. Through the smoky hallway, you see Chewbacca, mouth wide in a snarl as he reloads his bowcaster.

You must load your stunner first.

To reload your stunner: Your skill# +2 is your confront#. Roll the 6-dice.

If your confront# is equal to or more than your roll#, add the difference to your MP total. When they say that "the hand is quicker than the eye," they're talking about your hands.

If your confront# is less than your roll#, subtract the difference from your MP total. Chewbacca takes a quick shot, and you have to jump aside. Repeat the confront until you can reload.

The big Wookiee roars in defiance. Right now, you desperately wish that there was a way out of this ship. Unfortunately, Chewbacca is blocking the only exit.

You can try to put Chewbacca to sleep using Power, or you can stun him.

To put Chewbacca to sleep (using Power)*: Choose your Sleep Power. Your Power# + your Power's mid-resist# +1 is your confront#. Roll the 6-dice.

If your confront# is equal to or more than your roll#, add the difference to your MP total. The Wookiee drops to the floor and lies like a rug. You will not have to stun Chewbacca, and may proceed.

If your confront# is lower than your roll#, subtract the difference from your MP total. You must fight the Wookiee (below).

****Note:*** This counts as one of three Power uses you are allowed on this Mission.

To fight Chewbacca: Your weaponry# plus your weapon's mid-range# is your confront#. Roll the 6-dice to fight Chewbacca.

If your confront# is equal to or more than your roll#, add the difference +3 to your total. It was a solid hit, but it takes more than that to knock down a Wookiee. You must stun him again (below).

If your confront# is less than your roll#, subtract the difference from your MP total. Repeat the confront until you hit Chewbacca.

To stun Chewbacca again: You hit Chewbacca once, but the huge Wookiee doesn't go down. Instead, he drops his bowcaster and staggers toward you, anger raging in his eyes. You've heard about the horrors of Wookiee hand-to-hand combat. They specialize in ripping off people's arms and legs. You can't let him reach you. You back up a step and fire again. Your weaponry# + your weapon's short-range# is your confront#. Roll the 6-dice.

> *If your confront# is equal to or more than your roll#,* add the difference to your MP total. Chewbacca drops with a howl. He is safely stunned. You may proceed.
>
> *If your confront# is less than your roll#,* subtract the difference from your MP total. Repeat the confront until you hit Chewbacca.

The corridors of the *Falcon* are choked with so much smoke from the gunfire that you can hardly breathe. You drop low to the ground and head for the cockpit.

At that very moment, the *Falcon* lifts into the air with a rush. "Help!" you hear the golden droid shout, as it goes tumbling to the floor down in the access corridor. The little astromech droid squeals in terror as it is upended.

You wonder what is going on. Is Solo mad? You'd expected him to come and join the fight!

You lurch to your feet and rush toward the cockpit. When you reach it, Solo is sitting there, casually looking at you. You can see the scene ahead easily. The ship has reached an altitude of several thousand feet, and is now hovering perilously, nose pointed down toward a fiery volcano. You can see the flaming red of hot magma roiling within the mountain peak.

Solo smiles at you as beads of sweat dot his forehead.

He has his hand on the emergency power cutoff button, and has already pressed it. If he lets go, the power to the *Millennium Falcon* will shut down, and the ship will plummet into the volcano.

"So," Solo says, "it looks like I win again."

"I don't think so, Rebel scum," you answer.

Solo shrugs. "You've got a gun to my head, and in my own way, I've got a gun to yours."

"Don't let go of that button," you warn.

At that moment, the golden droid comes running up behind you. "Sir, Artoo-Detoo has fallen over, and I can't get him upright!" he shouts. Then the droid sees the monitor over your shoulder and says, "Oh my!"

"Look," Solo says, "I've got nothing to lose. If I go with you quietly, the Imperials will drag me off for some long slow torture, then give me and my friends a public execution.

"On the other hand, if I crash the ship into the volcano right now, I save both myself and the Empire a lot of trouble. And the really good part is that I get to take you out with me."

"There's always the hope of escape," you answer. "You could escape the Empire."

"Fat chance," Solo says. "You, on the other hand, definitely have something to lose. I'm willing to make you a deal. You drop your weapon and put on those restraints you have dangling from your belt, and I'll drop you off somewhere close to Caross. By this time tomorrow, you'll be sucking ice-cold varanta nectar through a straw."

"Why should I trust you?" you ask, considering whether you should shoot him now. There is a slim possibility that if you did, you could power up the ship before it crashed. But you're not at a very high altitude. That chance seems more than slim — it seems nonexistent.

"Hey, I'm a nice guy," Solo answers. "Everyone who knows me agrees."

"You're a scoundrel!" you answer.

"Rebel hero, Rebel scum — the only difference is which side you're on. Come on, you don't really want to die with me, do you? I mean, I shot you guys down, and by all rights, you should be etelo burgers by now. But you had to have gone through all kinds of work just to stay alive. I'm willing to bet you want to keep it that way."

You don't answer. Instead you consider the reward money that you see slipping from your fingers.

"On the count of three, either you toss your weapon over here, or we're all going to fry," Solo warns. "One. Two. Three."

"Oh no!" the droid shouts frantically.

You refuse to drop the weapon, calling his bluff.

Solo releases the power switch, and all the panel lights go dim. Immediately, you hear the ship's engines stop, and feel the ship begin to plummet.

Your heart pounds fiercely.

"We all gotta die sometime," Solo says.

You drop your weapon and lunge for the ship's power console, hoping to land the *Falcon* in a controlled crash.

As you do, Solo leaps up to meet you, swinging his fist. The blow is so unexpected you don't have time to react. It catches you full on the jaw and knocks you to the floor.

As you lie there in a daze, Solo reaches up and slaps a panel above his head. Suddenly, all the running lights return, and the ship lurches as the engines kick in.

Solo leans over you triumphantly and clasps the restraints onto your right wrist, then twists your wrist behind your back and hooks up your left wrist. You feel weak in the knees, and sick. Your ears are ringing and your sight is blurry. You've never been punched quite so hard.

"Hey," Solo laughs. "Looks like your lucky day. We aren't all going to die after all!"

Solo looks up at the droid. "Threepio, do me a favor and sit on this scumbag for me."

"I really don't think that's such a good idea," the droid says. "I fear that all of the excitement has overwhelmed my circuits."

"Sit down!" Solo says, pushing the droid onto your chest.

The droid says, "I'm really sorry about this. I really don't require leg rest, like you humans do."

Solo returns to his seat in the cockpit and pilots the ship down to the surface. You can hardly breathe with the weight of the droid on you.

"You knew we wouldn't crash!" the droid exclaims.

"I knew there was a short in my wiring," Solo answers. "Sometimes a punch to the access panel up there can do wonders. The risk was worth it."

You see Solo massaging his wrist. "Hope I broke it for you," you say.

"Save the insults, buddy," Solo says. "Maybe they'll come in handy next time we meet."

He gets up from the cockpit and loosens his blaster in its holster. He pulls the droid off of you, grabs the back of your shirt, and drags you down the corridor to the hatch. You wriggle to your knees, trying to stand, but your feet are still weak. He lowers the gangplank, and while you are sitting there, he gives you a good kick.

You go tumbling down the gangplank to land in the dust, staring up at Solo in the darkness. The hatch lights show his face. Your mouth is dry with fear, knowing that if Solo had any brains, he'd go ahead and shoot you now, putting an end to this.

The droid hurries up behind Solo, "Sir, you aren't going to shoot the bounty hunter, are you?"

Solo draws his blaster half an inch from his holster and saunters down to the end of the gangplank. As he stands over you, he says, "You know, if I weren't in such a fine mood right now, I'd really be tempted."

"I'll get you, someday!" you warn Solo.

"Probably so," Solo answers. "If not you, then someone like you."

At that moment, you see something small and brown wriggle up behind the droid.

It's Grubba. You'd forgotten about the Hutt in all the excitement.

In the dim light, you see something flash as Grubba raises your stunner and takes careful aim at the Rebel scum.

"Master Solo, watch out!" the droid shouts.

Solo draws his blaster and pivots, searching for a target.

Now is the time to strike, to spoil Solo's aim.

To spoil Solo's aim: You throw yourself at him with every ounce of energy. Your strength# +1 is your confront#. Roll the 6-dice to hit Han Solo.

If your confront# is equal to or more than your roll#, add the difference to your MP total. Solo gasps and tumbles over.

If your confront# is lower than your roll#, subtract the difference from your MP total. Repeat the confront until you hit Solo.

Grubba fires, and the blue bolt flashes into Han Solo's chest. He falls backward with a gasp, landing almost on top of you.

Grubba smiles triumphantly at you, huge golden eyes flowing. "If I let you live to suck another breath," the young Hutt says, "I get half the bounty on these Rebels."

"It's a deal," you say.

No one ever said it would be easy to capture a Rebel hero. You have captured Solo and his cronies, and within minutes you call the Empire to announce the news and claim your reward. Award yourself 250 MP (350 MP for Advanced Level Players).

The After-Mission

The Imperial Star Destroyer *Valiant* was not a huge ship, Leia thought as she watched it approach on the view screen in the crew's bay of the *Millennium Falcon.* It was only an old *Victory*-class Star Destroyer, smaller and sleeker than the new Imperial Star Destroyers. Yet no ship she had ever seen frightened her half as much.

Her heart beat in her chest like something caged, struggling for release.

The bounty hunters had reached the meeting point early, as had the Imperials. Obviously, the Imperials were in a hurry to retrieve the prisoners, and the bounty hunters wanted their reward.

Leia, Luke, Chewbacca, and Solo were all cuffed and shackled, sitting against a wall. The bounty hunters had drugged the Wookiee, Luke, and Solo, so that the men could not fight. They nodded their heads in a stupor. Even the droids had been fitted with restraining bolts.

No one was awake but Leia. No one could save them but Leia.

She struggled to pull her hands from the restraints, but the bounty hunters were using the highest-quality goods. Even as she struggled, metal cords in the restraints sensed her movement and clamped tighter.

Grubba the Hutt was at the gaming table, playing a holo game with Eron Stonefield. The young Hutt looked over at Leia and laughed. "I love to watch you struggle against your cuffs. It's like . . . watching a bug struggle in a spider's web. It makes me hungry."

"Always glad to entertain company," Leia said.

Leia looked at Eron Stonefield, and whispered, "Help me! You can't do this. Every time one of us Rebels dies, the hope for freedom that burns in the heart of every person in the Empire dies a little bit, too."

Eron glanced over her shoulder. "Maybe," she said. "But I'm not going to be able to buy an awful lot of freedom with this bounty."

Leia shook her head. "You've seen what the Empire is doing — plundering whole systems to power its war machines, enslaving those too weak to oppose it, and murdering those who are strong enough to fight. If you turn us in, you'll be a part of all that."

Eron's face was red with shame. Leia knew that she was getting to the young bounty hunter, that she almost had her.

Eron said, "The Empire would not clamp down so hard if the Rebels did not oppose it."

"You're wrong," Leia said. "If we did not oppose it, the Empire would have us all in its grasp. It's only because we fight that there is any hope for us at all."

Eron looked away, over to the cot where Dengar slept. Perhaps she was considering whether to set Leia free. Or perhaps Leia only imagined it.

"You must have family," Leia urged. "Brothers, sisters. Perhaps someday you'll even have children of your own. When you condemn me to death, you condemn them to slavery. Please — Dengar is sleeping. Do the right thing."

Leia wished then that she had the powers of the Force. She wished with all her heart that she could persuade the young woman. But Eron only sat, looking at the holographic monsters on the game board as they leapt across the squares.

"Do it now," Leia said. "Free me. The *Falcon* is a fast ship. Fast enough to outrun that old cruiser."

Eron Stonefield looked up at Leia, and there were tears glistening in her eyes.

At that moment, the *Falcon* shuddered as the Star Destroyer caught them in its tractor beams. The Imperials weren't going to take any chance that the *Falcon* would escape them this time. The *Millennium Falcon* seemed to be hurtling toward one of the big ship's docking bays.

"It's too late," Eron said. "I couldn't help you now if I wanted to. The Imperials have arrived early. There is no time left."

Leia sighed as the *Falcon* slowly drew into the docking bay. The bounty hunter was right. No one could help her now.

It was a proud moment in Dengar's life, though he felt no pride. The Imperial surgeons had cut that away from him, when they'd stripped him of emotion. Still, he felt a profound sense of accomplishment as the Imperial procession marched to the docking bay of the *Valiant* to take the Rebels prisoner.

Dengar and the other bounty hunters brought the prisoners to the bottom of the gangplank, while a dozen stormtroopers dragged each of them away — Han Solo, Chewbacca, the Princess Leia Organa, Luke Skywalker, and their droids.

The Imperial captain of this Star Destroyer, a young man named Fordwyn, was an up-and-coming officer whom Dengar had heard of by reputation. He presented a fine figure in uniform.

"Dengar, Stonefield, Udin, I would like to congratulate you on your fine work," Captain Fordwyn said, saluting each of them in turn. "The Empire owes you much. The capture of these Rebels will gratify the Emperor, and more important, it will teach those Rebel traitors that no one is above the law. The networks are already buzzing with news of the capture. This will make all of you famous."

As the captain spoke, Dengar watched the stormtroopers drag away the captives. The males were all drugged, but Leia tried to break free, and one stormtrooper threatened her with the butt of his blaster, shouting, "Get back in line!"

Then the stormtroopers left the bay, and Captain Fordwyn remained with his aides.

"Speaking of how much the Empire owes us, there is a small matter of the reward," Dengar said.

"Of course," Fordwyn said. "I have the credit disks right here. You have received the full rewards, and the Emperor himself asked me to give you a bonus. You'll find the Empire *quite* generous."

He handed over some computerized credit disks, and Dengar held them a moment. A bonus? he wondered. He felt torn between curiosity and concern. He was not a trusting person, and wished that he had a reader handy, so that he could see how much was on each disk. Still, it would have shown poor manners to do so in front of the ship's captain.

"Thank you," Dengar said.

"The capture went well?" Fordwyn asked.

"Aside from a little scuffle outside the palace in Caross," Dengar said. The Togorians of the Mindnight Fire clan had suffered a couple of casualties in the battle with the guards, and after the *Falcon* had blasted off, everyone had to run for cover. It hadn't been easy for the Togorians and the remaining bounty hunters to escape the city.

Fordwyn gazed at Dengar with steely gray eyes, and clapped him on the shoulder. "This is a proud moment in history. On behalf of the Empire, I thank you. I thank all of you. The Emperor will want to hold a reception in your honor. I trust you'll be free to visit Coruscant in the near future."

Dengar nodded. He'd made time for a trip to the Capital of the Empire for a party in his honor. "Yeah, but first I have some other business to take care of." He would not mention Jabba's reward to the Empire. Jabba was not one of the Empire's most highly regarded citizens.

"I understand that your ship needs immediate repair," Fordwyn said. "You'll be needing transport. I have a small shuttle that you can use. It will take you wherever you need to go."

"Oh, I won't be needing a ship," Dengar said. "I've got the *Falcon* here." He nodded to the ship behind him.

Fordwyn shook his head. "That old piece of scrap? I can't allow you to keep it. These Rebels have been trading in Imperial secrets. My orders are to confiscate the craft, strip it, and send the parts to sector security. There may be contraband aboard, or coded messages hidden in the computers."

That was a blow to Dengar.

"We do have a scout ship that I could loan you." Fordwyn nodded toward an old scouting vessel.

"Thank you," Dengar said, imagining he could buy a much greater ship with his reward — as well as repairing the *Punishing One*.

Fordwyn saluted. "It's yours, then. Until we meet again."

* * *

Two days later, Eron Stonefield and the others touched down on Tatooine. The sky was clear and sunny as they brought Grubba the Hutt before the great lord, Jabba.

Jabba slithered down from the Hutt throne, hugged the Ur-Damin, and then slapped young Grubba hard across the face. "How dare you let yourself get kidnapped!" Jabba said. "The reward money I paid will come from your future earnings!"

Grubba laughed. "Then you can have most of it back now. I won eighty-five percent of it from the bounty hunters. Given another game at the sabbacc tables, I could have won it all!"

Jabba smiled appreciatively at the Ur-Damin. "You make your predecessors proud!" the elder Hutt said.

Then Jabba looked up at Dengar, giving him a cold stare that chilled Eron to the bone. "You had Han Solo. You could have brought him to me for the reward."

"We gave him to the Empire," Dengar said. "Their reward was higher. Though I would hope that his capture satisfies your honor — enough so that you, too, will pay your proffered bounty."

"You didn't catch him. You gave him back into the hands of *Rebel agents*!" Jabba shouted. "You fools!"

Eron glanced from Dengar to Udin. "What do you mean?" Udin asked. "They gave us the credit disks. We checked them ourselves."

"Forged credit disks, no doubt," Jabba said. "They will land you in prison the first time you try to use them. The news is all over the nets."

Jabba nodded, and one of his henchmen flipped on a

monitor. It showed the scene in Mos Eisley as a reporter said, "Two days ago, the galaxy heard the sobering news that bounty hunters on Togoria had finally captured the Rebels who destroyed the Death Star. Now, we see the local reaction to the news that those same bounty hunters were duped into handing the Rebels over to Rebel agents disguised as Imperials."

In the city of Mos Eisley, the camera panned across the domes of the city. Moisture farmers were out dancing in the streets and shouting in celebration at news of the Rebel escape, for Luke Skywalker was a local boy. Jawas were throwing sand in the air, and the noise of cheers was so loud that Eron almost felt as if she could feel the vibrations in the air even here, in Jabba's palace.

Eron stared in shock. She could hardly believe it. A few days before, when she had given the Rebels into the hands of the Imperials, it had taken all of her will to do it. Capturing the Rebels had been a challenge. But sending them to their deaths had seemed . . . small and evil.

In her mind, she tried to put the pieces together, to discover how they had been duped. After the capture, Dengar had transmitted a message to the Empire to announce that he had Han Solo and his cohorts. That message had been picked up on all of the news nets. Only minutes later, the Empire had responded by sending a message, stating the time and place where they were to meet to exchange the prisoners.

The Rebels must have learned the time and location of the rendezvous point. The Togorians would have picked up the message easily, and they must have forwarded it to Rebel agents, who sent their own ship in. Dengar had been eager to off-load the prisoners and get his reward, so he'd shown up early, just as the Rebels had hoped. Eron realized that by the time any real Imperial ship reached the rendezvous point, the bounty hunters had already gone into hyperspace, headed for Tatooine.

"We lost them again," Dengar said, crestfallen. "Solo must have known the meeting point. He had them time the announcement to coincide with my arrival."

Jabba the Hutt laughed heartily. "A worthy adversary indeed! I always liked Han Solo. Too bad I will have to kill him."

The fifteen percent reward that the bounty hunters would get for Grubba was small pay indeed. Enough perhaps for Dengar to fix up his ship, enough for Eron and Udin to live on for the better part of a year, if they each lived frugally.

Small reward. Dengar seemed furious, but as Eron watched the monitor, saw the celebrations in the streets of Mos Eisley, she realized that people would be celebrating like this on hundreds of thousands of worlds. The heroes of the Rebellion had escaped!

Perhaps we failed, she realized. *And in doing so, we won more than we had dreamed.*

Yet Dengar raged and muttered under his breath, "It's not over, Han Solo! Someday . . . we shall meet again."

NEXT MISSION: REVOLT OF THE BATTLE DROIDS